Date Due

MAY 8	APR 30		
MAY 22	JUL 2		
June 5 '97	JUL 16		
JUL 2	AUG 11 98		
JUL 17	SEP 25 98		
AUG 2	DEC 24		
AUG 2 0	JAN 28 '00		
	MAR 6		
SEP 4	JUN 25 05		
OCT 31	SEP 19 03		
NOV 2			

4/97

Jackson
County
Library
Services

HEADQUARTERS
413 W.Main
Medford, Oregon 97501

The Missing Sunflowers

BY Maggie Stern

PICTURES BY Donna Ruff

 Greenwillow Books, New York

Acrylic paints were used for the full-color art.
The text type is Leawood Medium.

Text copyright © 1997 by Maggie Stern Terris
Illustrations copyright © 1997 by Donna Ruff

Printed in Hong Kong by South China Printing Company (1988) Ltd.
First Edition   10   9   8   7   6   5   4   3   2   1

Library of Congress Cataloging-in-Publication Data
Stern, Maggie.
The missing sunflowers / by Maggie Stern ;
pictures by Donna Ruff.
p.   cm.
Summary: Simon gets three sunflower plants
from his bird-loving neighbor Mrs. Potter,
only to have them disappear one by one.
ISBN 0-688-14873-5
[1. Sunflowers—Fiction.   2. Birds—Fiction.]
I. Ruff, Donna, ill.   II. Title.
PZ7.S83875Mi   1997   [Fic]—dc20
96-7148   CIP   AC

For Dan
—M. S.

For my own little boy
—D. R.

Simon wanted one thing: a garden of sunflowers.
Huge sunflowers that would tower above his head.
"It's too much work," said his mother. "You won't
take care of it."
"Oh, but I will," Simon said. "I'll do everything."
"Gardens are for girls," said his younger brother,
Jack.
"I want one," said Simon.

It was summer vacation, and Mrs. Potter, who
lived next door, had to go away for a few days.
Simon called her "the bird lady" because she
had eight bird feeders hanging on the trees
around her tiny pond.

"Simon, dearie," she said. "Can I impose on
you to feed the birds and carry in my mail?"

"Sure," said Simon.

"And, oh," added Mrs. Potter, "make sure the
squirrels don't snitch all the birdseed."

The next evening Simon found a large brown paper bag on the front step. A note said:

Dear Simon,
These are for you.
for feeding the birds.
Thank you.
Affectionately,
Hope Potter

Simon took three plants out of the bag. They had dark round heads with long yellow petals. "Sunflowers!" he bellowed.

Simon planted the sunflowers right in the
front yard. The largest, the one in the center,
bobbed its head. He stroked its soft petals.
"They look like lions," Jack said. "I want one."

"Come see what I've done," Simon shouted
as Mrs. Potter stepped out of her car four
days later.

"You certainly have a green thumb, dearie."
Mrs. Potter smiled.

Simon looked down at his thumb.

"It's just an expression," said Mrs. Potter.

"It means you have good luck with plants."

A few weeks later Simon began day camp.
Early that morning he sat in the yard pulling
out weeds. "Go away." He flicked a beetle off
one stem. "Don't touch my plant!"
Seeds were beginning to form near the petals
of the sunflowers.
The bus driver honked his horn.

After camp Simon was first off the bus. He ran to his garden.

The tallest sunflower was gone! Slashed off right under its yellow head.

Gone.

The heads of the other two flowers drooped toward the ground.

"Somebody cut my flower!" screamed Simon.

Jack and his mother came running from inside.

"Why, it's outright murder!" declared his mother.

"Who would do such a thing?"

Simon kept a lookout.

"I never imagined something like this would happen," Mrs. Potter said. "Not in this town." When the mail carrier dropped off the mail as usual, Simon carefully eyed his satchel. Just the right size to hold a large flower.

The next day Simon kept his fingers crossed.

As he hopped off the camp bus, the two sunflowers
seemed to nod their heads in greeting.

He stood in between them. "You've still got a ways
to grow to catch up to me."

"How about going out for ice cream?" suggested
Simon's mother one August afternoon.
When they reached home, Simon dropped his
cone on the brick walkway.
"Not again," he cried. He raced to the corner,
searching up and down the street.

"Mom, there's another missing sunflower!"
yelled Jack.
A girl on a blue bicycle whizzed by. Something
flashed in the basket on the handlebars.
"I'll find out who did this," Simon said.

Mrs. Potter came over the next morning.
"Dearie," she said, "would you be interested in
a job? I need regular help cleaning the feeders."
Simon nodded.

In one week Simon scrubbed all eight feeders.
The sunflower shimmied as he dashed back and
forth between the two houses. He stood on tiptoes
and ran his fingers across the rough seeds.

On the last Saturday in August Mrs. Potter was
in her yard.

"Come see this red-winged blackbird," she called
to Simon.

"I see one!" shouted Simon. He pointed across
the pond. "What's that yellow bird over there?"

"That's a finch," said Mrs. Potter.

She pulled a book and a pair of binoculars from her knapsack.

"Here, dearie," she said. "See how many kinds of birds you can find. The book is yours, and I'll lend you the binoculars for the rest of the summer." She hung them around his neck.

Simon sat on his steps, birdwatching, all the next morning.

A deep red bird landed on a branch. A worm dangled from its beak.

He dashed inside and found the bird book.

"No, that's not it. . . . No—yes! That's it. A—cardinal!"

He ran back outside, book and binoculars in hand.

The last sunflower had vanished!

Simon stayed in bed all of Monday.

Near dinnertime Mrs. Potter knocked on his door.

"Do you want the binoculars back?"

"Heavens, no," said Mrs. Potter. "I want you to get out of bed and see the blue heron in my pond."

Simon didn't move.

"Dearie, terrible things happen in life. But that doesn't mean you can stay in bed forever. Otherwise we'd all be there. Now get up and come see the bird."

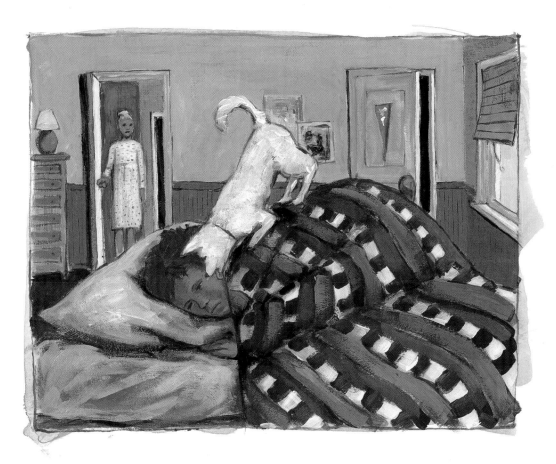

Slowly Simon followed Mrs. Potter into
her backyard.
The heron was gone.
"Snooze, you lose." She laughed.

That was when Simon spotted a trail of yellow petals at his feet. On hands and knees he followed it across the lawn.

As he reached the maple tree in the corner
of Mrs. Potter's yard, his hand came down
on something large, brown, and crumbly.
It was the mangled head of a sunflower!
"Somebody wrecked it," Simon wailed.

Simon flung himself onto the lawn. He felt
something hit his forehead.
He wiped away his tears and peered toward the
upper branches of the tree. He saw a gray, fuzzy
tail. Falling to the earth below was a shower of
crumbs. He knew those crumbs. They were the
shells of sunflower seeds.

"Mrs. Potter," he said, jumping
to his feet, "I've found the thief."
Mrs. Potter's eyes followed Simon's
finger. In silence they stared up into
the tree.

"Dearie, it's the way of nature."
Mrs. Potter put her arm around him.
"Squirrels have scissor-sharp teeth. It's
how they survive."

"I *hate* that squirrel," Simon cried. "How
dare it kill *my* sunflower!"

"Perhaps the squirrel thought that it was *his*
sunflower," said Mrs. Potter. She stood up.
"Sometimes the most precious things are
the ones we can't keep."

At supper Simon's father roared with laughter.
"I'm relieved," said his mother.
Through the dining-room window the sky was
turning crimson. There were two bluejays on
one of Mrs. Potter's bird feeders.
Simon sighed.

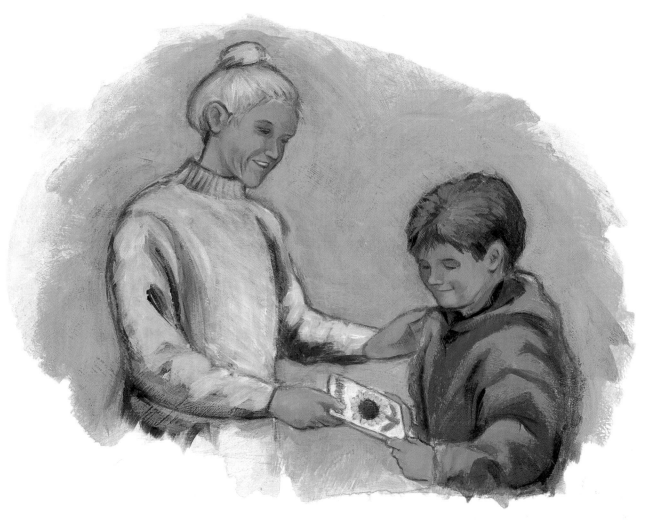

The following morning Mrs. Potter dropped by.
"I have a little something for you."
Inside the bag was a package of sunflower
seeds.
"You can plant these next spring," she said. "And,
dearie, I read in my gardening book that a dash
of red pepper will keep the squirrels away."

That afternoon Simon gazed out his window.
The stalks below were still. There, at the tip
of one cut-off stem, a new bud had sprouted.
Simon smiled. He looked toward Mrs. Potter's
yard. Resting in her pond was a large bird with
a long neck.

"A blue heron," he said in a whisper.

He watched as the great bird slowly spread its
wings and took flight.

Simon took a few sunflower seeds from the bag
that Mrs. Potter had given him.
He opened his window and one by one placed
the seeds on the outside ledge.
"For the heron," he said. "Or for any bird."

He would give Jack the budding sunflower.

Simon picked up the bag of seeds and went into the kitchen. He found a jar of red pepper on the spice rack. Standing on a stool he put the jar and the seeds on the top shelf of the cupboard. He was set.

Simon ran into his yard, binoculars thumping against his chest. Spring was a long time away, and right now the birds were calling.